Marina Yankelzon

Remembering Gustav Klimt

50 ABSTRACT PATTERNS IN THE STYLE OF THE ART NOUVEAU MASTER

In today's world, where stress and tension are becoming an integral part of everyday life, more and more adults are looking for ways to relax and enjoy creativity. One of the popular methods of dealing with stress has become coloring - anti-stress for adults. And if you are looking for something special that can immerse you in the world of art and beauty, then the coloring book "Remembering Gustav Klimt" with 50 abstract patterns in the style of the master of Art Nouveau is just what you need.

About the magic of coloring:

Coloring is not just a hobby or a way to spend time, it is a whole process that can bring harmony and peace to your life. When you immerse yourself in the world of creativity, you forget about everyday worries and problems, devoting yourself entirely to the creative process. Coloring abstract patterns in the style of Gustav Klimt will not only help you relax, but also immerse yourself in the amazing world of modernism and symbolism.

The art of Gustav Klimt in every detail:

Gustav Klimt is one of the greatest artists of the Art Nouveau era, his works are full of symbolism, mystery and beauty. Each pattern in this coloring book is designed taking into account the style and technique of Gustav Klimt, so that every color, every line and shape brings you joy and peace. You will be able to color the famous circles, spirals, zigzags and other elements that are so characteristic of the work of the great master.

The coloring book "Remembering Gustav Klimt" with 50 patterns in the Art Nouveau style is not just anti-stress, it is an immersion in the world of art, an opportunity to feel like a part of a great creation. Allow yourself to plunge into an atmosphere of beauty and inspiration, forgetting about problems and worries, and discover new facets of your own creativity.

The coloring book "Remembering Gustav Klimt" is a fascinating journey into the world of art and beauty that can bring you peace and joy. Immerse yourself in the symbolic and mysterious world of the Art Nouveau master and enjoy the creative process that will help you relax and get inspired. Don't miss the opportunity to transform your time and space with a coloring book that can reveal your inner artistic potential and bring new bright colors into your life.

Made in the USA
Las Vegas, NV
29 November 2024

12887631R00057